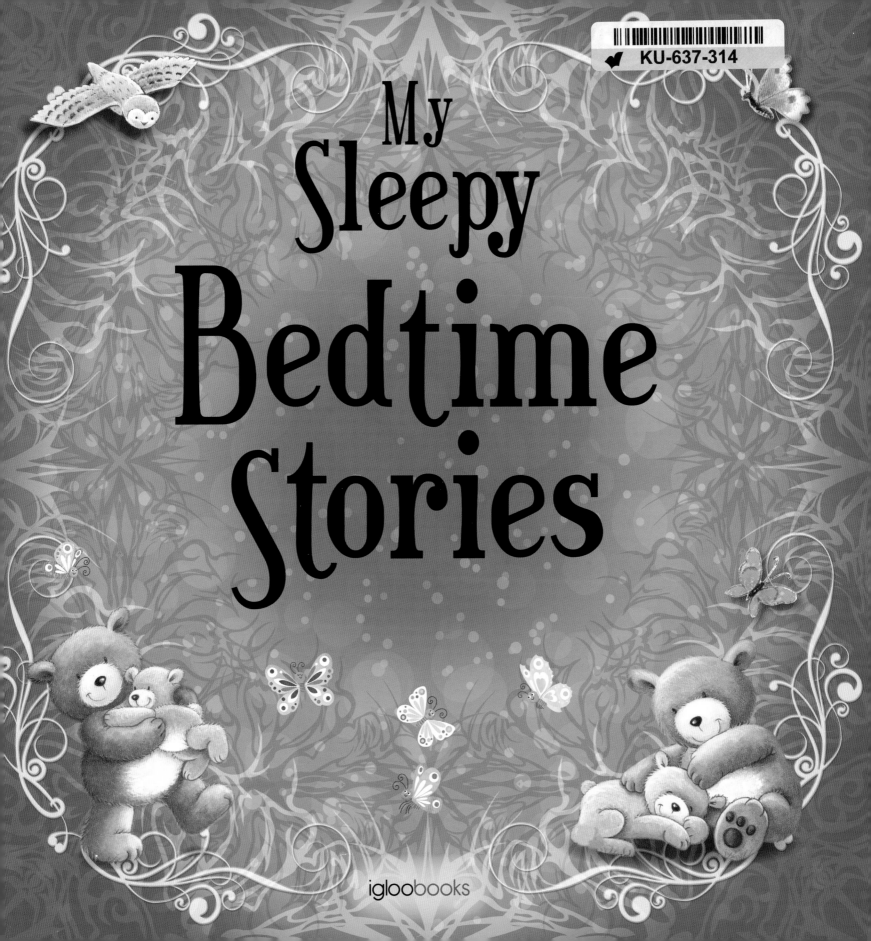

My Sleepy Bedtime Stories

igloobooks

Contents

Goodnight, Little Bear

Little Bear was feeling sleepy. It was nearly the end of the day.
His mum had come to take him home. There was no more time to play.

This igloo book belongs to:

....

igloobooks

Published in 2013
by Igloo Books Ltd
Cottage Farm
Sywell
NN6 0BJ
www.igloobooks.com

The measurements used are approximate.

FIR003 1113
2 4 6 8 10 9 7 5 3 1
ISBN 978-1-78197-146-8

Illustrated by Helen Rowe, Karen Sapp and Gareth Llewellyn

Printed and manufactured in China

Little Bear yawned and gave a stretch. “I feel a bit tired,” he said.
Mum took his tiny paw in hers and gently stroked his head.

“All little bears get sleepy,” said Mum, “and the sun is sinking low.
It will soon be bedtime for everyone. It’s time for us to go.”

Little Bear gave his mummy a cuddle, in the rosy evening light.
"Can I go to see my friends?" he asked. "I want to say goodnight."

Little Bear said goodnight to the birds, twittering in their nest.
They fluttered their wings and chirruped, then settled down to rest.

Mother Duck quacked to her ducklings and they cuddled under her wing.
"Goodnight," said Little Bear to them, as the skylark began to sing.

Mum and Little Bear went to the stream where all the fish swished.
Little Bear said goodnight to the frogs as they happily splashed and splished.

“I’ve had a lovely day,” said Little Bear, “and it’s been lots of fun.”
“Goodnight,” he said to the foal dozing under the setting sun.

"Goodnight," said Little Bear to the butterflies, fluttering in the breeze.

He said goodnight to the fluffy
squirrels nestling in the trees.

"I wish you sweet dreams," said Little
Bear to the sleepy, soft dormouse.

"Sleep tight," he said to the baby bunnies curled up in their cosy house.

Along the shadowy woodland paths, the meadow bees came humming.
"They are flying back to their hive," said Mum, "because the night is coming."

“When will night be here?” said Little Bear. “Will it be coming soon?”
“Yes,” replied Mum, “and then you will see the stars and shining moon.”

Little Bear looked up into the sky and the glowing sun had gone.
In its place were twinkling stars and a round moon brightly shone.

“The stars are magic,” said Little Bear and he gave a sleepy yawn.
Then he said goodnight to the dozing deer and the little fawn.

"Come on," said Mum. "It's getting late and you're a tired little bear."
Very gently, she scooped him up and softly said, "There, there."

Little Bear felt very tired. He gave his mummy a sleepy hug.
"We'll soon be home," said Mum, "and you'll be nice and snug."

Soon, Little Bear was safely home and ready to go to bed.
He chose a bedtime story and then he snuggled down with Ted.

Before the story was over, Little Bear's eyes began to close.
Mum just looked at him and smiled, then kissed his little nose.

At last, Little Bear was fast asleep and in the world of dreams.
His bedroom was filled with starlight and silvery, soft moonbeams.

"Goodnight, Little Bear," said Mum. "Sleep safely through the night.
I will watch over you and keep you safe until the morning light."

Goodnight, Little Bear. Sweet dreams.

Bear's Magic Moon

Little Polar Bear's home is cold and snowy. The icebergs glimmer, the water sparkles and Little Polar Bear plays with her friends all day long.

Little Polar Bear loves rolling in the crisp, white snow until her fur sparkles and she loves diving into the blue, swirly water to chase fish. There's just one thing that Little Polar Bear doesn't like.

The night. It is very, very...

... DARK!

Tonight is a very special night and all the polar bears are gathering to welcome the full moon. “Come with me, Little Polar Bear,” says Daddy. “It will be great fun.”

"We will sing songs.
We will dance until the sun
rises over the icebergs.

We will dive in the water
and chase the sleepy seals,
then the Wise Old Bear will tell us about his adventures."

Little Polar Bear is too scared of the dark though, so Daddy goes to welcome the new moon by himself.

"I'll never be able to welcome the new moon," says Little Polar Bear.
"I'm just not brave enough."

Big tears roll down her nose and plop onto the ice.
Then, she hears a heavy paw-step scrunching in the snow.
Little Polar Bear is very scared!

It's only the Wise Old Bear! "Don't cry, Little Polar Bear," he says. "There's nothing to be afraid of. Come outside and you will see something wonderful."

Little Polar Bear shivers and shakes, but she goes outside with the Wise Old Bear. Little Polar Bear is frightened.

But slowly...

... slowly...

... slowly...

... she looks up.

The round moon is full and bright.
“It’s so beautiful,” whispers Little Polar Bear.

"The moon and the stars are your friends," says the Wise Old Bear. "You can tell them all your secrets. They have watched over bears for hundreds and hundreds of years and they will watch over you, too."

Little Polar Bear runs to meet Daddy. "You're here," he says. They jump and dive and play in the water.

They sing and dance in the moonlight.

Daddy gives Little Polar Bear a big bearhug.
“You did something very special,” he says.
“You did something even though you were scared.
Do you know what that makes you, Little Polar Bear?”

"The bravest bear of all!"

Bedtime, Little Bear

Late one afternoon, Little Bear was balancing on an old log. It was a good game.

"Time for bed, Little Bear!" called Mother Bear. "It's getting late!"

Little Bear stopped balancing for a moment... and fell off! He didn't feel a bit sleepy.

"I don't think that could have been Mother Bear calling me," he said to himself. "It must have been the trickling stream."

A few minutes later, Little Bear found some lovely leaves to play in. His friend, Mouse, passed by.

"Little Bear," called Mouse, "I think I heard Mother Bear calling you."

Little Bear poked out his head. He didn't want to stop playing. He was having so much fun!

"I don't think that could have been Mouse's squeaky voice," he said to himself. "It must have been the rustling leaves."

When Little Bear finished playing,
he noticed that the sky was as red and gold as
the fallen leaves he had been playing in.

He climbed a tree to get a better view.

High in the branches, his friend, Squirrel, was scampering past.

"Little Bear!" called Squirrel. "Didn't I hear Mother Bear and Mouse calling to you?"

Little Bear hugged the trunk. "That wasn't Squirrel calling," he said to himself. "It must have been the breeze swishing through the trees."

Little Bear watched as the sun slipped behind the hill. Then he climbed down to the bottom of the tree.

Shadows were deepening all around him.
"It's time to go home," said Little Bear.

As Little Bear trudged through the trees, the moon rose up into the sky and all the twinkling stars came out.

"It's almost as light as day," said Little Bear. Somehow things looked different at night and scary, too. Little Bear wasn't sure which way to go.

Now, Little Bear thought that maybe someone *had* been calling him. He wished that he had answered. What if he could never find his way home?

Just then, he heard a tiny sound... "Little Bear!"

Little Bear listened harder.

"Little Bear! Little Bear! Little Bear!"

"That's not the trickling stream," said Little Bear.
"It's not rustling leaves, or the breeze in the trees.
It sounds like Mother Bear!"

It was! Little Bear ran right into
Mother Bear's warm, furry arms.

Mouse and Squirrel, who had been helping Mother Bear search for Little Bear, did a little dance of delight.

Little Bear felt very sleepy now, so Mother Bear carried him home to his snuggly bed.

"Goodnight, Little Bear," said Mother Bear, softly.

"Goodnight, Little Bear!" called Mouse
from his comfy bed.
"Goodnight, Little Bear," said Squirrel
from his treetop nest.

It was peaceful in the woodland
and all that could be heard
was the trickling stream…
… and the rustling leaves…
… and the breeze in the trees…
… and a little bear snoring, softly.

"Goodbye,

see you soon!"

Activities

Now that you've finished reading, why not complete these fun activities?

Let's start with a close-up challenge.
All of the close-up images below are in this book.
Can you find them and write down the number of the page they are on?

a.

b.

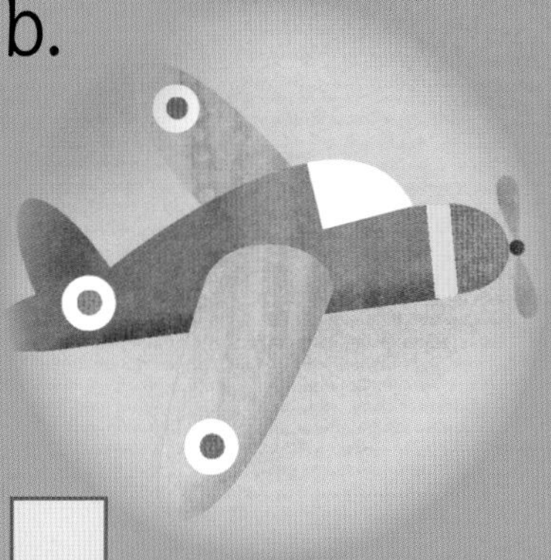

c.

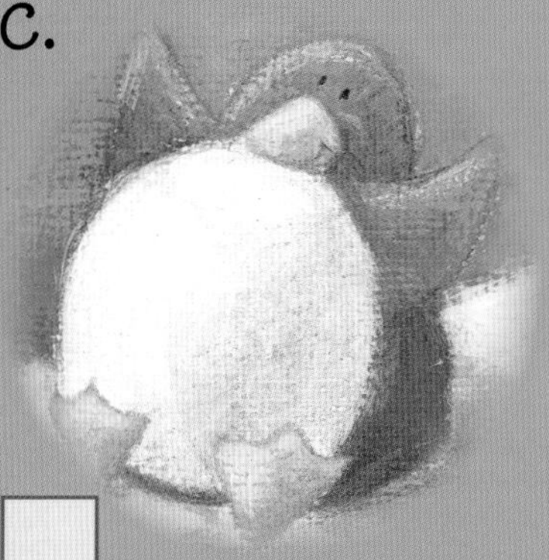

d.

Now, which of these images is the odd-one-out?

a.

b.

c.

Answers are on page 72

Activities

How closely were you paying attention to the stories? Can you answer all of these questions correctly?

1. In *Goodnight Little Bear*, how was the evening light described?

2. In *Goodnight Little Bear*, what did Little Bear say to Mother Duck and her ducklings?

3. In *Goodnight Little Bear*, where were the bees flying back to?

4. In *Bear's Magic Moon*, what does Little Polar Bear not like?

5. In *Bear's Magic Moon*, who comes to visit Little Polar Bear in her cave?

6. In *Bear's Magic Moon*, who does Little Polar Bear run to meet?

7. In *Bedtime Little Bear*, who passed by when Little Bear found some lovely leaves to play in?

8. In *Bedtime Little Bear*, who did a little dance of delight?

9. In *Bedtime Little Bear*, where was Squirrel when he said goodnight to Little Bear?

Answers

Close-up Challenge: a= page 8 b= page 28 c= page 35 d= page 67

Odd-one-out: B (Little Bear's Mum is missing her hair bow, see page 20)

Answers

1. rosy (page 11) 2. goodnight (page 13) 3. their hive (page 20)
4. the dark (page 37) 5. Wise Old Bear (page 42) 6. Daddy (page 46) 7. His friend, Mouse (page 56)
8. Mouse and Squirrel (page 67) 9. from his treetop nest (page 69)